IF YOU
LISTEN

IF YOU LISTEN

GUNILLA B. NORRIS

illustrated by Dale Payson

Atheneum   1971

New York

8463

For Jane Persen
because she listens

IF YOU
LISTEN

FROM THE APARTMENT WINDOW Lia watched the big car being packed. It was time to leave the city for the summer. It wasn't because the apartment was too hot and cramped either. The truth was she could yell from the kitchen and Mrs. Stark, the housekeeper, wouldn't hear her in the living room. No. The apartment wasn't a bit cramped. It was huge and fashionable, in fact, with high ceilings and foot thick walls. And it was located in the right part of the city.

Lia wrinkled her nose. The William Strattons wouldn't live anywhere else. Well, at least Mother wouldn't. Sure, Mother'd go to the country in the summertime. It was the thing to do. Especially since they owned a big country place. And there Mother could take more of her pills because Father wouldn't see her do it. He'd only come to the country on the weekends once in a while.

Lia pushed her fiery hair back. Sometimes . . . sometimes she wished she could talk to Father or just . . . well, be with him. Lia bit her lip. Father was loud and scary. Sometimes she really was afraid of him. Still she wished he were home. If nothing else, when Father was home Mother didn't dare take all those pills.

Lia had seen Mother pack the vanity case this morning. It was full of little plastic bottles containing pills —tranquilizers she'd heard Mother say once. Mother had looked up. She had seen Lia watching her. But Lia had hurried away to her room. She hadn't let on she had seen anything. Lia didn't dare speak to Mother about the pills. Somehow she just couldn't. There were lots of things you couldn't talk about. It was as if Mother would just look at you, cool and polite and sort of miles away, and it always made Lia feel like . . . like she was all wrong somehow. And then it was impossible to talk. Maybe that was why Father didn't say anything about the pills to Mother either.

Lia shivered in the cold air conditioning. She lifted the blind and looked out the window again. The car was almost ready. Soon it would be time to leave.

Lia picked up her things. She wasn't excited about going. It didn't matter where she was, in the city or in the country, things at home were just the same.

Lia sighed and started towards the door. Well, at least she had something in the suitcase she cared for. Something nobody in the house knew about. She'd keep it a secret, too. You could bet your life on that.

Softly Lia closed the door, the way Mother said she had to, and walked out. Now she could hear Mrs. Stark calling her. Lia grabbed her suitcase tighter. It was time to go.

I

SHE WAS IN THE COUNTRY. Her room was beautifully decorated with bold painted furniture, with yellow chintzes and a fluffy fur rug. Lia turned around in it. She sniffed. It smelled dusty and new at the same time, a smell she knew so well. Every place she lived in was like that, including the apartment. It was a store smell, the odor of things on display, belonging to no one in particular. Lia frowned. Why did nothing ever smell old and loved and used? Nothing except Noni.

Lia leaned down and dug into her suitcase where she had hidden her treasure. She always had to wait until she was alone to take it out. Quickly she fished in the suitcase. Out came a fuzzy, bedraggled, no-colored owl with one shiny button eye. Lia put her face against him, breathing in the smell. She sighed. Noni always had to be hidden, tucked under pillows and into corners, under mattresses or stashed deep in a drawer beneath a pile of underwear. Lia closed her eyes and held the owl close. She was too old for him she knew. If the housekeeper, crisp and sensible Mrs. Stark, ever found him, she'd throw Noni into the nearest garbage can. If Mother found him, she'd turn cold and distant, her forehead clouding over with disapproval.

Lia smiled the sad lopsided smile that she knew revealed all the metal wires of her braces. Pills or no pills, Mother was always disapproving. She had Lia's curly hair uncurled just so. She had Lia's teeth straightened. She made her daughter take gymnastics for posture, French lessons for culture. Too bad there was nothing one could do about her freckles that were scattered like galaxies on the firmament of Lia's cheeks, or her long legs, straight like tomato stakes!

Lia sat down on the perfectly smooth bedspread. The bed squeaked a little protest. She held Noni closer. Sometimes she didn't feel real. It was as if Mother and Mrs. Stark and even Father had dreamed her up, cutting her into shape like a paper doll, furnished with a full wardrobe and Jeannette, a

paper doll friend just like her.

Billy, Lia's brother, always laughed at her. "For Pete's sake," he'd say, "don't be a twirp. Don't listen. Don't pay attention. Why do you have to go around believing all that?"

Billy was lucky. Being older and a boy he somehow escaped the whole thing. And anyway, he refused to be William Stratton, Jr. He was always dirty and loud on purpose, with pockets full of junk just to exasperate Mrs. Stark.

Lia sighed. Well, maybe he didn't escape. But he seemed so sure and ready to fight every minute. Often Mother just gave up and let him off. But Lia wasn't a bit sure. She went around feeling scared and . . . and . . . as if she had to do what everyone said.

Lia stiffened. She cocked her head. Did she hear Mrs. Stark coming up the stairs? A fearful prickle ran down her arms. Quickly she stuffed Noni in a boot and threw him under the bed. She dove for her suitcase.

"Lia dear?" Mrs. Stark opened the door. "Oh, good, you're unpacking. When you're done, come straight down for a bite. We're going to fatten you this summer. You're far too thin."

Lia grunted.

"You know your mother doesn't want you to grunt. Please answer properly. And don't dawdle."

9

"No, Mrs. Stark," said Lia and made a face into the suitcase.

She waited what seemed endlessly for the door to close. Then silently she snaked under the bed to fetch Noni. Lia lay there a moment.

"Never," she whispered fiercely to the owl. "She's never going to find you. Never."

Lia wrapped the toy in a sweater and thrust it deeply back on the closet shelf behind the extra blankets. Then Lia unpacked her things, placing several items on the shelf. There! Nobody would find Noni.

She went across the huge room to the window. Below lay the yard with its closely clipped grass and then the meadows and the woods. The woods weren't part of the property, but all around the large stone house were acres of open land. Lia sighed. It was so different from their apartment and yet things at home were always the same.

Lia's eyes narrowed. Maybe this summer would be different. Lia gazed at the large elms at the farthest edge of the meadow. They beckoned with their leafy arms, and rising behind them, were the hills thrusting up, up into a distant blueness. Maybe she'd go up into the hills this year. Billy said there was a lot to explore there. Maybe if Billy went with her she'd dare. Maybe . . . Lia wrinkled her freckled nose. Billy wouldn't like that. He liked to go off by himself.

"Quit tagging along. Give a guy some space."

Lia spun on her heels. Who was she kidding? This summer wouldn't be different at all. Father would be away most of it, and Mother had her vanity case full to the brim. Lia cast a last longing glance at the closet shelf, and then with lips shut tight and lopsided, she plodded resignedly down the stairs.

II

"DARLING, SUCH A FACE," said Mrs. Stratton.

Lia looked away from her mother.

"I know you're tired after the long ride from town. We all are. Sit down and have a cucumber sandwich, dearest."

Lia sat down at the large mahogany table. I hate cucumber sandwiches, she thought and stared at the roses in the wallpaper.

Her mother watched her and then sighed wearily. "Very well, don't have a cucumber sandwich. But you *must* drink your tea."

"Where's Billy?" asked Lia and looked her mother straight in the face.

Mrs. Stratton was a thin woman with great shadows behind her eyes as if she were constantly backing into hiddeness. The rest of her, though, sparkled with cleanliness and good grooming. Lia had never seen her mother mussed or perspiring. She was always cool, glittering and not quite present.

"Where's Billy?" repeated Lia, gulping her tea.

"Don't gulp, Lia. *Please*. You know Billy's out there somewhere." Mother waved a thin hand towards the window. "There's no holding him. What he does I can't imagine."

Lia looked out the window. "I don't know either," she said wistfully.

The silence settled uneasily between them.

"Is Daddy coming for the weekend?" asked Lia cautiously.

Her mother dabbed her thin lips with the linen napkin. "He will if he has time," she said swiftly.

"Oh," Lia answered and gazed down at her reflection in the shiny surface of the table. She looked a little like Daddy. But she wasn't sure. He was so rarely home. Sometimes she thought she couldn't remember what he looked like.

When Daddy was there he was followed by a wake of noise and movement. Around him nothing stood still or was quiet. It seemed so strange after all the silent time with Mother. And Lia didn't know how to be with him. He scared her a little with his big thunderous laugh and his strong red hands that would swing her around a room the way you did a toddler. Still, she wanted to be scared that way.

Daddy had been a farm boy, a self-made man, as he put it, and proud of it. Sometimes he'd look at Billy and shake his head.

"Little whippersnapper. Never have to do a solid piece of work in a day. You don't know how lucky you are," he'd say. "When I was young I never even had a new pair of shoes."

Then Billy would clamp his lips together and stare at his feet. Lia could almost tell what he was thinking.

"Who asked to be your son? Who wants to ride around in expensive cars and have people point at you? That's William Stratton's son! It's hard even to have a real friend who's your very own friend and not somebody trying to make a fuss over you because of your father."

Lia thought maybe that's why Billy spent so much time by himself. It was easier. You didn't have to be on your guard every minute.

Lia watched her mother get up from the table.

"I'm going to rest," she said.

For a minute Lia couldn't help but frown. She knew Mother was going to take some pills now. Then she'd get all silent and drifty and far away. More far away than she usually was. Lia looked at Mother. She looked little and frail. Sometimes Lia wished she could hug her. But you just couldn't hug mother. She was neat and cool and perfect in that distant way, and then Lia just couldn't. Well, they had never been huggy together anyway.

Frowning, Lia rose and hurried towards the door.

"Don't go too far away, Lia," said Mother after her. "Be on time for dinner. I don't want you all tired out the first day."

"O.K., Mother," said Lia softly and slid out into the late glow of the afternoon.

The air smelled sweet and rich. Lia shook her red hair into a mass of those unwanted curls. She ran through the tall meadow grass. It tickled and scratched her long thin legs. She picked a daisy and started plucking.

"She loves me . . . She loves me not . . ."

Hastily Lia counted the petals ahead. They weren't going to come out right. Lia dropped the flower, not wanting to finish the game. Instead, she slowly plodded to the fence and sat on it under the dappled light of the elms. Always there seemed to be a hollow pinch down deep inside her. It made her feel as if she were alone in a dark deserted place, and it was so even if there was sunlight, even if the birds sang and called above her head.

"Oh well," she sighed and thought of Noni deep and snug in the secret corner of the closet.

Lia turned and looked into the rising woods behind her. They seemed a little dark, mysterious and secret. Lia swiveled on the fence and let her long legs slither down the split rails. She stepped into the shadows of the trees. It was quieter here than in the meadow. There was no drone of bees and the birds seemed silent. Her foot snapped a twig in half. At the noise gooseflesh rose on her arm. Lia shivered nervously.

Where was Billy, she wondered? Lia peered into the trees and walked further. She turned her head frequently to be sure she could still see the meadow and the house below.

The wind rose now, whistling softly through the trees on its way to some distant place.

Lia stopped. Her heart was beating. She'd never been this far before. Lia cleared her throat.

"Yoo-hoo!" she called out with a soft hiss. Then louder, "YOO-HOO!"

It was a loud, pent-up sound, breaking out through the trees and echoing far away into the hills.

All at once a twig snapped. Lia twisted about. She saw something move. It was white and pink. It was red and brown. Lia cried out in fear. It ran off, dashing up towards the ridge of the hill. It was gone. Lia crouched and watched after it with wide eyes. But she only saw the leaves bobbing on the bushes. Then a remote sound of twigs breaking drifted back to her. Lia heard her breath come shallowly.

What was it? A deer? Lia swallowed and closed her eyes. No, it hadn't been a deer. Deep inside she knew it hadn't been. It had been a person. Lia was sure of it. A girl.

III

"Yoo-hoo! Yoo-hoo!"

Sue-Ellen heard Lia's cry. She stiffened there in the fork of the old tree. The cry startled her though she had been watching all along as the girl climbed the wooded hill. She had noticed the mass of red hair spilling all over the girl's head. She had seen the thin face shine white and vulnerable like a willow stick bared of its bark. Then the girl's call had come suddenly, loudly. Something glinted in the girl's mouth.

Sue-Ellen stiffened. Then quickly she jumped to the ground. It was as if she had been flushed out of hiding. Suddenly she had to run, dashing away over the top of the ridge and down the other side, plunging through the woods up and over the next rise.

Twigs snapped under her feet. She scraped her skin on a stump. Still she ran because it felt right. It was what the deer did, running long after the danger was over, because it felt good. The summer wind blew her wispy blond hair. The leaves crunched softly beneath her bare feet. She scared a chipmunk into his hole and ran till she came to the meadow below Granny's house. There Sue-Ellen flung herself in the tall meadow grass and panted.

Her head was filled with the loud banging of her pulse and the sight of the turning blue sky like a pinwheel in a breeze.

Slowly her breath came back. Sue-Ellen giggled and rolled over on her stomach. It had been exciting. A little tickle of fear still ran in her blood. But she felt safe in Granny's meadow. From here she could see the porch surrounded with hollyhocks and the chicken coop out back. Up there at the height of the meadow was safety and all that she knew: Granny, Zenas, their big yellow tom cat, the cantankerous chickens and the black water of the brook brown by the dirt road with its constant singing and spilling off into mystery.

Sue-Ellen sighed and wondered about the other girl. Was she from the big stone house way down below? Was she as old as Sue-Ellen herself? She allowed her curiosity to be for a moment. It was like a small frightened rabbit, ready to run and be gone. Sue-Ellen twisted to her back again. If the girl was from the stone house, there was no call to think on it anymore. Sue-Ellen blew noisily through her nose. Probably the girl was. And that was the end of that.

Sue-Ellen stood up. She had a sudden need for all that was familiar, warm and sure. Quickly she snatched at the daisies as she went. She'd make Granny a pretty nosegay and find a fresh egg for Granny's supper.

With urgency Sue-Ellen hurried up the steep meadow, trailing daisies and foxgloves.

"Granny!" she called "I got you a nosegay."

She slammed the screen door behind her. The old woman sat in a rocker in the late sun, mending.

"I got you a nosegay," repeated Sue-Ellen, planting a hasty kiss on the old woman's wrinkled cheek.

Granny smiled. "Well, thank you, child."

"Want I should find the eggs?" asked Sue-Ellen, plunging the flowers in a milk can. She set the can on the worn kitchen table.

Granny nodded and watched Sue-Ellen carefully. It felt almost as if she could read into her, as if she could read the very thoughts in Sue-Ellen's head.

"Did you have a scare, child?" asked Granny slowly.

Sue-Ellen wormed her way to the door. "Not 'xactly!" She didn't want to talk about it. Quickly she let herself out through the screen door.

Sue-Ellen ran to the hen shed. Carefully she looked in the loose hay for the hidden eggs. It was powerful and strange the way Granny knew everything. Sue-Ellen chewed on her lip. Sometimes it was a comfort. Granny would know all the hurts and fears before she ever spoke them, or knew them herself even. It was a mystery. But Sue-Ellen thought maybe when you were as old as Granny you just knew, knew from plain living. Still, it was strange. Often in the winter, when the kids in the school laughed at her for being strange and shy; when she couldn't stand up to recite for the knocking in her knees; or read even when she heard the words yelling at her in her head, then Granny knew. Sue-Ellen didn't have to tell her. They'd sit quiet and safe by the old kitchen table and let the hurt fly off, silent like a spider's webb in a breeze.

But sometimes Sue-Ellen wanted to keep a thought, to be turning it in the dark as she waited for sleep to come or when she felt the loneliness of being just Sue-Ellen and Granny and Zenas and the chickens. Then she didn't want Granny to know.

Sue-Ellen plunged her fingers into the hay and found an egg. It was still warm. She cradled it in her brown stubby hand and drifted off a moment.

Was the other girl her age, would you suppose? Lord, what a lot of red curls, bobbing like fool's gold on a body's head! Sue-Ellen fingered her chin. And what were those silver things on the girl's teeth? . . . Certain, there was no end of things to wonder about.

IV

LIA'S SKIN PRICKLED. Whatever she had scared was gone now. Lia turned around and plunged down the wooden hill to the edge of the meadow. She saw Billy crossing the graveled path to the house.

"Billy!" she yelled, hoping for an answer. But she was too far away. She dove under the fence and ran to the house.

It seemed suddenly dark and quiet inside. The lights hadn't been turned on yet. Lia stood in the hall listening. Faint noises could be heard from the kitchen where Mrs. Stark was preparing dinner. Billy was in his room. Mother was still "resting." Lia wrinkled her nose.

Then she crept up the dark stairs like a shadow. She knocked on Billy's door.

"Billy," she whispered.

He let her in quietly. She saw he had a toad in his hand.

"Don't tell Starky," said Billy, "and shut the door. I'm going to keep him in the closet. I'm just looking for something to put him in."

"Won't he die?" asked Lia and frowned.

"Well, there's more out there."

"Still," said Lia, "he should be free. He's wild and . . ."

"Don't be an old sissy," said Billy. "What's a little toad?"

Lia closed her mouth. She saw the toad puffing, the pulse beating by its bulbous eyes. Then it leaped to the floor. Billy dove after it and grabbed it.

"Don't hurt it!" cried Lia.

But Billy only smiled. From his fist came a soft squeaky noise. The sound made Lia shiver. She spun on her heels and ran to her room. Behind her she could hear Billy laugh.

Lia shut her eyes and pushed her palms against her ears. Sometimes she didn't like Billy. Sometimes she didn't like anybody. Lia squeezed her eyes shut. If only she could hold Noni for a moment. But Mrs. Stark would come any time now to call them for supper. Lia didn't dare get him out of the closet.

Lia rocked on the bed and closed her eyes. She shivered remembering the strange thing that happened this afternoon. Had it been a girl she had scared, Lia wondered? Maybe it had been something wild? Lia bit her lip. At least whatever it was got away—scared but still free.

It made her think about the toad again. Maybe she'd go into Billy's room and let the toad loose. Maybe when Billy wasn't looking she'd dare. He'd be mad, but it'd be worth it. She wouldn't care how mad he was. Lia pinched herself and swallowed. Then and there she promised herself she'd do it.

It was the next day after breakfast. Billy had gone off again. Lia watched him head down the gravel drive. Once out of sight Lia stole into Billy's room. The closet door was shut. Silently she opened it. Inside it was dark. Lia felt along the floor. Suddenly something in a box moved. Lia let out a little startled cry, but she reached into the box after the toad. She had to grab it hard.

"Poor thing," she said, clutching it close to her chest.

The watery eyes bulged up towards her.

"I'll hurry," she whispered. "Don't you worry."

Lia plunged down the stairs and ran to the meadow.

"There!" she said, setting the toad down. "Hurry. Go. Go!"

The toad didn't move.

"Please," cried Lia urgently. "*Go!* Billy might come back!"

Still the toad just sat.

Lia pushed him. Then he hopped weakly into the tall grass and Lia spun on her heels. But there was Billy staring at her.

"You let my toad go!" he yelled, turning red.

Lia took a step back.

"He was so little," she blurted out, "and, and besides . . ."

Billy ran into the meadow. He parted the grass in a frenzy, but he couldn't find the toad.

"I'll teach you!" he cried and tore into the house.

Lia ran after him. He raced off to her room, ripping the door open. Without a word he opened her bureau drawers and emptied them all over the floor. Pants and sweaters fell into a jumbled pile.

"Stop it, Billy!" cried Lia glancing desperately at the closet. "You haven't any right to wreck my room."

"You should have thought about that before you let my toad go."

"That was different!"

Billy dashed to the closet and in one great sweeping

motion he pulled everything off the shelf.

Lia saw Noni come tumbling down to the floor, lying mangy and exposed among the blankets with the one black button eye staring up at the ceiling.

"Children! Children! What's going on?" Out of breath Mrs. Stark ran in. "Stop at once!"

Lia could see Billy grin triumphantly. He gave the mess on the floor a swift little kick and was out the door.

Despairingly Mrs. Stark glanced around. Lia held her breath.

"Please don't let her see Noni," she pleaded in her head. "Please."

But Mrs. Stark bent down and picked up Noni where he lay.

"What's this?" she asked, holding the toy in her hand at a distance.

"No-nothing." Lia swallowed.

"Gracious," said Mrs. Stark. "It must have been left over from some summer visitor or other. I'll take it. You clean up, Lia. And no more fights. I'll speak to Billy."

"Please . . ." Lia took a step forward. But by then Mrs. Stark was half way down the hall.

Lia slammed her fists in the bed. Blackness welled up inside her. Noni was gone. Gone. She banged her head on the mattress, again and again. She didn't hear anything. She didn't see anything.

Then slowly she became aware of Billy in the doorway. She twisted away from him and all of a sudden the tears she'd kept back came rushing forward.

Billy watched her. "Come on, Lia," he said taking a step forward. "I didn't know you still had that old owl."

Lia shook her head and couldn't speak.

"Why'd you have to let that toad go? I wouldn't have . . ."

Lia sobbed, holding herself. She couldn't hear him for her own crying.

Billy shifted from foot to foot. "Come on, Lia, stop. I'll find it for you. There's got to be a way to get it back. Starky's no magician."

Lia gave no answer. She only whimpered harder.

Billy cleared his throat. "I'll go," he said and spun around.

Lia jerked her head up. Through blurry eyes she looked for Billy, but he was already gone.

V

Lia came down the stairs much later. She'd soaked her face in cold water, but it was still blotchy. In the living room Mother looked up from her book. Lia could see a frown pass over her face like a dark cloud over the far distance of the sky. Lia turned away. She went outside into the bright sunlight.

For a moment the light pained her tired eyes. She stood feeling strange and lost without anything to do and think. She just stood, faintly hearing the crickets in the meadow grass.

"Psst, Lia!" Billy waved to her from behind the carefully sculptured planting at the corner of the house. "Lia!" He raised his voice to make her hear.

Slowly Lia turned. Billy waved to her urgently. "I've got him. Hurry!"

For a moment Lia blinked without understanding. Then she grasped what Billy was saying. She ran to him.

"Where?" she said. "Where is he?"

Billy thrust a crumpled paper bag into Lia's hand.

"It was already on the pick-up truck. I had to think up a lulu to tell the man to let me look through the trash." Billy was flushed with his adventure. "I found an old pocket knife, too. And the man said he'd let me ride with him sometime . . . maybe."

But Lia didn't listen to him. "Thanks, Billy," she murmured and turned.

Lia knew what she had to do. Holding the bag carefully, she ran straight across the meadow towards the elms and the woods beyond. Breathless, she crawled over the fence. The woods seemed soothing to her, cool and gentle to her eyes. The dappled green light fell like a comforting cloak over her. Lia slowed down, walking softly in the crackling leaves and holding the precious bag tightly to her chest.

She'd have to go far in to be safe from Billy, safe from everyone. She was going to find a hiding place for Noni where no one, no one at all would find him.

Lia walked on, up, up, over the first ridge and the second. It was growing warmer. Lia brushed the sweat from her upper lip. She wanted to stop, to look at Noni, just to sit and touch him.

At last she couldn't hold out any longer. She had to stop. Lia nestled in the leaves beneath a big maple. Almost reverently she opened the bag. Noni lay face down, an egg shell still clinging to his matted fur material.

Horrified Lia grabbed him up and shook him free of the bag and all that clung to him. He looked terrible. Lia almost cried. But at the same moment she was flooded with relief. It was still the old Noni, and Lia loved him. Gently she held him, letting all the stored and secret love she had to give pour out. She didn't speak; she just held the little gray bundle and tried to feel whole again. Lia closed her eyes. She could stay there forever in the dappled woods, feeling the warmth of Noni's fur and hearing the squirrels clicking in the thickets.

Sue-Ellen heard someone coming from far below. She herself was on the way to the berry patch. Granny had said she had a hankering for raspberries today.

Sue-Ellen stood and listened, the excitement mounting in her like a horse about to bolt. Sue-Ellen swallowed. She'd just maybe look to see who it was. If she went quiet-like no one would be the wiser.

Sue-Ellen edged down from below Granny's meadow and barefooted she hurried along the path, keeping the berry pail carefully ahead so it wouldn't bang or make a noise.

When the foot steps grew louder Sue-Ellen ducked into a pine thicket. She sat there, head pounding, when she saw the girl from yesterday come hurrying towards her. Sue-Ellen swallowed and pulled herself into a greater smallness. But the girl didn't pass. She sat right down in the leaves below the large maple. She shook something out of her bag. Sue-Ellen watched wide-eyed. She studied the girl's pinched face, saw it soften into love and gentleness for the gray bundle she held. Sue-Ellen watched. She watched the other girl close her eyes and slowly, slowly, drift into peacefulness.

Sue-Ellen licked her lips and a soft sense of knowing and wonder scudded across her face. She knew something now. She knew she wasn't afraid of this girl with the bundle. Even if she were from the big stone house, even if she were strange as a hedgehog in midwinter.

Quietly Sue-Ellen crawled from beneath the pine thicket. Then the berry pail clanged against a stone making a loud ring. Startled, Sue-Ellen looked at the other girl. Lia opened her eyes. They were big frightened bluenesses. Hurriedly, Sue-Ellen nodded.

It was a formal gesture but a little smile hovered about the corners of her lips.

Lia thrust Noni behind her. She swallowed.

"I reckon you fell asleep," said Sue-Ellen softly.

"Yes." Lia stood up, holding Noni behind her.

"I saw him," said Sue-Ellen, indicating Noni with her head.

"Oh!" Lia dropped her arm to her side. She gazed in confusion about her. "Who are you?" she asked. "Where'd you come from?"

"Up yonder," said Sue-Ellen. "And I reckon you're from below," she continued. "From the big stone house place, ain't you?"

Lia nodded. She pulled herself together. "I was just sitting here resting," she said. "That's not a crime, is it? And well . . . you needn't think I sit holding toys all the time."

The words rushed out of her, tight-lipped and hard. She couldn't stop them because she'd been jolted out of sleep and a private feeling.

Hastily Sue-Ellen turned. "I'll be going," she said, seeing the other was mean and scared now.

"Where are you going?" Lia demanded.

"To get some berries for Granny," said Sue-Ellen. Now she, too, wanted to get away. She felt strangely caught by this girl.

Lia ran and seized Sue-Ellen by the arm. "Promise

35

you won't tell about him." She indicated Noni. "If anyone should ask you. Promise?" Lia held the girl's arm in a tight grip.

"I ain't got cause to tell," said Sue-Ellen. "That's nothing to me." She felt a little frightened now. She didn't understand.

Lia let go. "I'm sorry," she said and turned her face away. "I didn't mean . . . well . . ."

Sue Ellen saw the other's face fall into itself with a kind of lostness, the way a kitten looks not finding its mother. Sue-Ellen cleared her throat.

"You can come if you like," she said nervously and pointed to the berry pail. "There's enough for two." Sue-Ellen didn't know where she'd found the courage to ask the girl. The words just rushed off by themselves like chickens on the loose.

Surprised Lia looked up. She blinked. Then solemnly she nodded.

"I'd like to," she said.

"Well, then . . ." Sue-Ellen started off.

"My name's Lia," said Lia hurriedly and followed.

"Lia," repeated Sue-Ellen. "Well then, you're welcome, Lia."

Sue-Ellen never broke her stride, needing the motion and the distance between them.

"What's yours?" asked Lia following behind. "Your name?"

"Sue-Ellen," said Sue-Ellen almost in a whisper. Suddenly saying their names had made her too shy to speak anymore. She started running.

VI

THEY DIDN'T SPEAK. All around them the raspberry bushes nodded and swayed in the wind. It smelled sweetly of heat and berries and greenery.

Lia cast a hurried glance at Noni propped safely in a nearby tree. She smiled inwardly and bent over the berries, dropping them carefully in the rumpled brown paper sack Billy had given her earlier.

On the far side of the patch the other girl picked in a silent hurry. Lia could feel Sue-Ellen didn't want to talk. They were two quiet stones in a brook, which the sun, the birds' chatter and the green smelling wind washed over.

The sun rose to its height. Lia brushed the sweat

from her forehead. She was tired. By now the bag was half full. She stood resting, putting a few berries in her mouth. Lia looked at the other girl. Would she never stop?

"Sue-Ellen," said Lia cautiously. "Can't we stop now?"

Sue-Ellen looked down at her brimming pail. "I reckon," she said reluctantly. Sue-Ellen looked across the berry patch. It would have been easier to go on picking. Lia seemed to be waiting for her to come. Slowly, shyly, she picked her way over.

"Great Scott, how'd you get so many?" asked Lia with admiration. In the stillness her voice sounded like thunder.

Sue-Ellen shrugged and looked away. She felt as if she'd like to bolt and run. But instead she walked with Lia to the shade and sat on a stone.

Once there Lia began to gaze at Sue-Ellen sideways. Her jeans were patched at the knees and Lia could see the frayed neck of the plaid shirt she wore. There were scratches on her arm and her straight blond hair hung in bunches. Sue-Ellen gazed straight ahead. Lia knew Sue-Ellen felt her staring. Lia looked down a little ashamed.

It was so awkward. What could she say to be friends? It was as if Sue-Ellen were nailed to the stone against her will. Lia frowned. It didn't seem right to ask questions. Lia sighed and turned away. They sat close but still so distant while the silence grew around them like a fertile thicket.

Then all at once Lia saw the doe. A little sharp excitement prickled up her arm. Silently, urgently she put her hand on Sue-Ellen's and pointed with her other. Out in the berry patch the doe saw the movement and froze.

Sue-Ellen and Lia sat suspended, holding their breath, holding each other's hand. Then slowly the doe lowered her head and began eating the raspberry leaves. Still the girls did not move, locked in a kind of magic circle with the doe. The animal moved closer and closer, eating the berries and leaves, nibbling with soft and nimble lips.

Lia felt her whole body grow warm with excitement and joy. Never, never had she seen a doe so close. Lia glanced at her companion. Slowly they grinned at each other, their hands feeling warm and safe in one another's. The larks fluttered high above in the sun-baked sky and the wind rippled through the berry bushes, washing over the red fruit, the green sweet leaves, and the two girls on their stone.

Suddenly they couldn't bear the silence, the caught suspended magic of the doe eating only yards away from them. The girls stood up on the stone.

The doe jerked to attention. Sue-Ellen glanced

at Lia. "Yoo-hoo," she mouthed and Lia nodded. Then in chorus like cocks in the early morning, they called out.

"Yoo-hoo! Yoo-hoo! YOO-HOO!"

It was as if it were an announcement, a statement of beginning. The sound leaped out of them, sending the doe hurtling off into the woods and breaking open the silent world.

VII

Mrs. Stark frowned down at Lia and turned to confront Mrs. Stratton at the dinner table again.

"The child's never where I can get her anymore. For two weeks now she's been off somewhere in the woods. Dirty. Unkept. She's never home in time for meals. She hasn't washed her hair in that time or had it cut and straightened for over a month now. I don't like to say this Mrs. Stratton, but I think something has to be done. And Mr. Stratton coming tomorrow evening and all."

Lia squirmed. She watched her mother's pale face. Mother had been absent the last two weeks, staying in her room on the chaise longue for a good part of the day. She had been far away and preoccupied and Lia knew she had been taking pills. Now Mother's eyes were brought back from that distance. She turned her head towards Lia and really looked.

"Mother, it's summer," began Lia in protest, seeing the critical look creep into Mother's face.

From the corner Billy watched silently. He was brooding over Father coming. A waiting sort of gloom settled over the table.

Mother opened her long-fingered hands. Her nails were like perfect oval jewels. She made a weary little gesture.

"Take them into town tomorrow, Mrs. Stark. Hair cuts for both. Get something for Lia to wear. Something light and summery. We can't have her looking like that!"

"Oh, Mother," cried Lia. "Can I have some jeans like . . . like . . ." but then she bit her lip on Sue-Ellen's name. She felt a sudden wrench because her mother's frown came deep and sharp like a knife into her hopefulness. It pierced suddenly into the secret life Lia had now in the woods. Mother made it feel ugly somehow. And it had been so wonderful.

Every day in the last weeks Lia had met Sue-Ellen under the big maple. They'd found a hollow tree to hide Noni in and they had private, elaborate games. Neither asked questions. It was as if they'd promised

43

each other not to ask about what was beyond the woods for either of them. They just shared the light and the shadow of the trees, the creeping of the small animals, the silent growing of the mushrooms, the endlessness of a summer day. Lia looked away. Mother's gaze shattered everything.

It was as if suddenly nothing good had happened. In her mind's eye Lia saw how Mother would see Sue-Ellen. Dirty jeans, disheveled hair, black, torn finger nails. She'd notice Sue-Ellen's voice, husky with "ain't's" and "reckons."

Lia swallowed. She felt suddenly cold. She rose from the table and hurried upstairs. Everything good broke or was taken away. Lia shut her eyes tight. Whatever Mother thought, Lia wouldn't let her spoil everything. She wouldn't. Nobody was going to. She'd die first.

Lia's scalp prickled from the shampoo and the hair straightening. Her body itched in the new blue organdy dress. She felt wretched and stared out the window down the dusky driveway where Father would drive up any moment. Listlessly she walked to the far window of the living room and looked towards the elms and the rising woods.

What had Sue-Ellen thought when Lia hadn't turned up today? What had she imagined while Lia was in the torture of the hairdresser? Lia swallowed apprehensively. She wondered about Noni, too. Was he safe in his tree?

Lia turned to gaze at Mother, cool and beautiful. Mother looked up briefly and smiled at Lia, sweeping her quickly with approving eyes.

"She doesn't see me," thought Lia. It came upon her suddenly, clearly. The idea wasn't strange. It had been there all along, though hidden. "She just sees the dress. She doesn't see me at all."

Lia turned away and stared at Billy. He sat silent, slapping a pack of dog-eared cards on the game table in an intense, private game of solitaire.

"We're in a cage," thought Lia, suddenly startled by her own thoughts. "A beautiful cage Father put us all in."

She watched Mother finger her hostess gown nervously. Lia realized that Mother was in a cage, too. Not just the one they were all in, but one made up of little clear plastic bottles as well. Lia heard the empty silence surrounding each of them. Everything was quiet like a night that went on and on and on.

Lia inched over to Billy. She touched him shyly on the shoulder.

"I'll play knuckles with you," she said almost in a whisper.

"O.K." Billy smiled fleetingly.

Then they heard the big car come up the drive. Father was home. Despite everything Lia felt a rush of excitement.

In a moment Father was inside the hall, filling it with himself.

"How's everybody?" he roared and didn't wait for an answer. He pulled Billy's ears, pecked Mother on the cheek and twirled Lia in a giddy circle. They were left dazed and breathless.

"Hope Starky's got a good dinner," he said blowing loudly through his nose and marched into the living room. Soon he was settled in the sofa with a large drink in his big red hand.

They all waited to see what was expected of them. Lia edged herself towards the window. She was waiting for something, hoping for something. She didn't know what exactly.

"Well, what have you been doing?" Father demanded.

"Oh, resting a lot," said Mother trying to sound animated about it. "The children have been doing quite a bit of exploring. Haven't you?" she said tensely, turning to Billy, asking for help.

"Yeah, a lot," said Billy.

"Good. Good. And Lia?"

"Well . . . well, nothing much . . . just . . ." She didn't know how to begin. The longing inside her

rose. She wanted to tell him, to share something.

But Father turned and stared out the window. Suddenly he wasn't listening anymore.

"Who's responsible for the meadow?" he declared and got up angrily from the sofa. "I asked for it to be cut two weeks ago!"

"Well, the man's had trouble with his machine," said Mother.

"Excuses. Every time."

"Can I go now?" asked Billy.

"No!" roared Father.

Lia felt gooseflesh rise on her arm.

"What's the matter with all of you? It feels like a morgue in here," said Father.

Mother laughed nervously. "Everything's so dead without you, dear," she said dryly.

Billy snorted and flopped down to his cards again.

"The children are off in the woods all the time and . . . well, things *are* quiet."

Lia could see Mother making a brave effort. Billy made a face. Lia could feel her tears come rushing up under her eyes. She wanted to run out into the woods and find Noni, to sit in the comforting dark and let the tears come weltering out.

"They don't need to be quiet. You could arrange for some house guests, couldn't you? What about the Symonsons? Don't they have a girl Lia's age?"

"Yes, Jeannette," said Mother with a brilliant, tight, little smile.

"And later there can be someone for Billy. They can be spaced," said Father. "I can get up for a few days in a couple of weeks."

"How nice, William."

Lia heard Mother's hostess gown rustle nervously across the floor as she went to stand by the window.

Then Mrs. Stark appeared in the doorway at last.

"Dinner's ready," she declared.

Father grunted and a little sigh of relief escaped from Mother. Lia swallowed. Her head pounded. She resisted the urge to run, run far off somewhere. Instead she walked obediently towards the dining room and the long dinner ahead.

VIII

SUE-ELLEN PACED the listing floorboards in the kitchen while Zenas stared at her from beneath the rocker. What had happened to Lia yesterday? Was she mad? Sue-Ellen bit her lip and stopped by the geranium in the window, stroking its furry leaves.

Was it happening again? Sue-Ellen narrowed her eyes. Had Lia grown tired of her the way the girls at school did, wearying because she didn't chatter and giggle. Sue-Ellen frowned. Lia hadn't come at all. Just up and disappeared!

Sue-Ellen didn't know what to think. She'd gone down in the woods. She'd waited in the shadowed light, waited by the tree where Lia's gray owl lay wedged in the hollow. She'd waited nigh on all day like a patient heifer in a pasture. Oh, but she was sore inside. A bad ache was growing in there all covered over with silence. Sometimes she felt like a leaf trembling in the wind, one of those that covered its hurts over with queer brown bumps and hardnesses.

Now Granny looked at her over her glasses, not saying anything. Sue-Ellen swallowed and sat down in the rocker. She pulled Zenas into her lap and buried her face in his yellow fur.

"You got cause for achin', child?" asked Granny softly.

Sue-Ellen shook her head. "No, I ain't," she murmured. "Nothin' anyway as I didn't expect."

"There's fresh buttermilk for you."

"No thanks, Granny." Sue-Ellen looked up at the old woman. "It ain't nothin'," she said trying to look her old self.

"Still it's hurtin' you, child. Seems only people can hurt people. You found someone out in them woods, didn't you, child?"

Sue-Ellen swallowed. How did Granny know? How did she? Granny seemed to know by just hearing your breathing. Sue-Ellen looked down and nodded.

"Well, child, somethin' might have happened. You give it a bit of time. A strayin' rabbit goes the round

51

way back to his hole."

"But Granny . . ." Sue-Ellen swallowed and then she blurted it all. How Lia and she had met. About the doe in the raspberries and the silent games under the leaves. Sue-Ellen sighed.

"Well," she said at last. "I reckon as she's from the stone house below . . . well, I reckon she's feelin' too good for playin' with the likes of me anymore."

"Mmmmmmmm," said Granny softly. "I guess you'll be findin' out soon. Maybe. . . . Supposin' she came back. Maybe, it'd be good if you brought her here."

"But Granny!" Sue-Ellen's eyes opened wide in panic. "I couldn't."

"Why not? Are you ashamed?" asked Granny and peered at Sue-Ellen. "Is it you, Sue-Ellen, that is thinking you're not good enough, not fit to play with? Is it?"

"No, Granny." Sue-Ellen swallowed and looked away. "Still and all . . ." She dug her hands in Zenas' thick fur. "Oh, Granny, I don't know. I can't make it out."

"I guess you can't," said Granny kindly. "Still, it's a sore thing, ain't it child? Sore and difficult."

Sue-Ellen nodded. She rose, letting Zenas drop to the floor and she went over to Granny. With gentle stubby fingers she stroked Granny's hair.

"I love you, Granny," she said fiercely and then

she bolted, flying out through the screen door and running down over the meadow.

At the breakfast table Lia squirmed in her chair. What was Sue-Ellen doing? Was she cross with Lia? Would she be by their tree? Oh, why didn't Mother excuse them all?

And all the while Lia felt the pinching of the organdy dress. She could hardly eat her breakfast. Father had already sent Billy to find out what was happening with the farmer who was to cut the meadow. Billy had been relieved and very quick about going. Lia had seen that he was wearing his oldest pants and his hair wasn't combed. But nobody said anything to Billy. Only *she* had to sit there in a blue organdy misery.

Lia couldn't wait a moment longer. She made a move to go. With a little frown Mother looked up. Lia froze.

"What are your plans for the day, dear?" Mother asked.

Lia shifted her feet. She felt a terrible uneasiness.

"I don't know, Mother." Lia looked down. She could sense Father's eyes on her.

"Speak up, Lia!" he thundered.

"I thought. . . ." She swallowed repeatedly. "I throught I'd go exploring a little."

"But your father's here," said Mother. "Shouldn't you stay around, love?"

"Everyone dashes to the woods when I arrive, is that it?" Father laughed a loud, dry laugh.

"Lia, you'd better stay here," said Mother swiftly.

"But Billy got to go," blurted Lia. She looked around wildly. She couldn't stay away from the woods another day. Sue-Ellen would never understand and then maybe she'd never come back. Never ever.

"Your father *asked* Billy to go," Mother pointed out. "Now sit down, darling and talk to your father."

Lia swallowed. She could feel the tears packing in under her lids. "But . . . but . . ."

"One day won't hurt that much, now will it?" laughed Father a little hollowly.

Lia stared at Father. So often she'd been waiting for him, hoping he'd come, hoping for . . . but now there was Sue-Ellen. Lia gulped air. Didn't Father care about that? Didn't he care about what was important to her? The truth was he didn't know anything about her. He wasn't ever home himself to find out. Lia felt a sudden sharp, fierce anger.

"Then why are you away all the time?" breathed Lia, her eyes widening with fear at what she was doing. "If you think that. If you think one day doesn't hurt." She gulped and nearly choked.

"Lia!" Mother half rose from her chair.

Lia plunged on, not caring what she said. "You keep us all here . . . like, like a cage. Locked up till you come to see we haven't escaped." A sob exploded from Lia before she could take it back. "And nobody cares. Nobody cares about anybody in this family. Nobody hears or listens to anybody. Nobody even sees who anybody is. What they're like or anything."

She was about to blurt out more, to say something about Mother's pills. But suddenly Lia felt cold with fear at what she had already said. She rose shakily and blundered out of the room to the outside.

IX

SUE-ELLEN HEARD HER COMING long before she saw Lia. Excitement and joy leaped in her. Lia hadn't stayed away. But Sue-Ellen's smile soon faded when she saw her friend. Lia's red hair stood out around her head like a red ball of flames. Teary streaks of dirt lined her freckled cheeks. Her dress had been torn and her legs had angry red scratches. Lia jerked Noni out of the tree and hugging him tightly she flung herself on the bed of dry leaves and sobbed.

Uneasily Sue-Ellen drew back. She watched Lia in dismay, but she still couldn't speak. Slowly Lia's sobs grew quiet. She rubbed her face against Noni, murmuring to herself. Slowly Sue-Ellen put her sturdy brown hand on Lia's shoulder. She could feel the other still trembling. Sue-Ellen gave her a little pat and waited.

Then at last Lia pulled herself up. She held Noni close to her chest, and looked at Sue-Ellen through blurry eyes, but she had to look away again. More tears wanted to come. Lia buried her face in Noni.

Still Sue-Ellen couldn't say a word. She felt as if her tongue were gone and there was nothing she could say. Uncertainly Sue-Ellen moved closer. She put her hand out and touched Lia's hair gently. Lia sobbed, but she let herself slowly, hesitantly lean against Sue-Ellen. They sat close together like that until at last Lia was quiet.

"Do you have a mother and a father?" asked Lia sniffing and turning towards Sue-Ellen.

Sue-Ellen's eyes widened. She swallowed. Now would come the questions. The questions that always came relentlessly somehow, sometime. The questions that spoiled everything. Sue-Ellen sat up stiffly. The truth was bare like a branch in winter. Her mother had died when Sue-Ellen was born. Her father she didn't know. There was only Granny. Sue-Ellen rose. The questions made her want to go off by herself.

But Lia had grabbed her arm and was waiting for Sue-Ellen to answer.

"No, I don't have a mother and a father," Sue-Ellen said at last and pulled her arm free.

"Then neither do I," said Lia fiercely. She stood up, tucking Noni under her arm.

Sue-Ellen turned. Lia's words were not what she had expected. Suddenly she didn't feel cold and shut off. Maybe . . . Sue-Ellen stood a long uncertain moment thinking of Granny, thinking of what Granny had said. "Maybe it'd be good if you brought her here." Maybe it'd be good . . .

Abruptly Sue-Ellen started off, walking up through the woods, up, up towards the meadow. Quickly, shyly she waved for Lia to come, and then she plunged on. Behind her she could hear Lia following.

Now Sue-Ellen's heart banged hollowly like a stone in an empty oil drum. She stood on the edge of the meadow waiting for Lia. Her skin prickled when Lia approached and stood squinting up at the old ramshackle house on the top of the hill. Sue-Ellen could see a chicken pecking by the porch.

Would Lia think it looked old and worn? Would Lia think she was too good for Sue-Ellen? . . . Sue-Ellen ducked her face and looked at her bare feet.

Lia waited for Sue-Ellen. But her friend didn't move. "Can we go up?" asked Lia at last.

Sue-Ellen swallowed. Slowly she nodded and then she set out on the narrow path of trampled grass through the meadow.

They reached the house finally.

"Granny!" called Sue-Ellen shakily on the porch. "Granny!"

Through the screen door Sue-Ellen could see the old woman stir from her nap in the rocker. Now she could also feel Lia standing behind her.

Granny came to the door, her white hair flying off in little wild wisps.

"Oh," she said. "Company. Come in." Graciously she opened the door. Granny smiled a near toothless smile and let Lia pass. Lia stared all around, seeing the bare wood floors, the room empty of much furniture. But it was warm, and somehow she didn't feel strange.

"Fetch some buttermilk from the cooler, Sue-Ellen," said Granny, "and there's some graham bread on the drainboard there. Go on child."

Sue-Ellen flew, glad to escape a moment. And Lia sank down by the kitchen table, smiling shyly.

"Granny. . . ." Sue-Ellen ducked back into the kitchen. "Granny, her name's Lia."

"Thank you, child," said the old woman and nodded. Slowly she pulled Zenas out from beneath the rocker. "This is Zenas," she said giving the old yellow tom cat to Lia.

Lia stroked his fur and grinned. She sat and waited for the old woman to speak. But it was silent for

59

a long while. Distantly she could hear Sue-Ellen rattling something. At last the old woman spoke.

"I think Sue-Ellen sets great store on your friendship," said Granny slowly. "You're always welcome here."

"Thank you," whispered Lia. She felt embarrassed but not uncomfortable because she did feel welcome. Then Sue-Ellen darted in, eyeing them both nervously.

"Here's the milk," she said plunking a metal pitcher down on the table. It still had beads of cold brook water on it. Quickly she set out glasses and the bread. "You can eat now," she said nodding and smiling shyly.

They all ate but no one spoke. It seemed strange and a wonder to Lia how they all did say something to each other though no one uttered a word.

At last Granny broke the silence. "It's a mighty hot day. Maybe you'd be liking to swim in the brook a bit." Granny nodded to them.

"Would you like that?" asked Sue-Ellen cautiously.

Lia nodded.

"Run along then. Mind, you don't freeze your toes off."

Lia laughed. "Thank you for lunch," she said bobbing her head and following Sue-Ellen out the door.

"You're entirely welcome," said Granny to herself nodding and smiling. She watched the girls go off and she sighed deeply. "Entirely welcome," she repeated softly.

Following behind Sue-Ellen, Lia thought of home. It had been in the back of her mind all along like a dark heaviness. Back home they'd wonder where she was. Lia shook herself silently. She was afraid of what they were thinking, of what they were doing; but still there was a spurt of anger in her. She wouldn't go home!

Lia dashed ahead to catch up with Sue-Ellen, to run from her thoughts and plunge into the brightness of the day and the moment.

"It ain't far now," said Sue-Ellen with a shy grin. "There's a right deep place not far off. And it's clear away from the road. I reckon that's the best." Sue-Ellen surprised herself. The words flowed easily. They came rolling out, all natural, not cranked out stiffly one after the other like buckets from the well.

The girls came to a standstill by the brook. It was a shaded place where sunlight only fell in patches and the trees grew thick and leafy.

"I reckon it's cold," said Sue-Ellen staring down at the dark brook and stirring the water idly with her bare feet. She began to unbutton her shirt.

Lia nodded. She suddenly felt embarrassed realizing they'd go skinny dipping. Lia looked down at her blue organdy dress and frowned. She shifted uncomfortably on her feet.

Sue-Ellen looked her full in the face. She sensed Lia's hesitancy.

"You needn't swim," she said hurriedly. "It might be too cold for you."

Lia swallowed. "No, it won't be," she said, setting her lips firmly. She reached for her buttons. Quickly she had crawled out of the scratchy organdy, flung her shoes and underwear to one side and splashed into the dark, slow moving water. It *was* cold.

Lia shrieked and splashed. In a moment Sue-Ellen raced in. The white sprays flew up with their giggles as they tried not to look at each other's nakedness.

But soon it grew too cold for them. Lia headed for a sunny flat rock that stood out of the water. She crawled up on it, hunching her shoulders around her knees. Sue-Ellen came and sat with her.

"It sure is cold," muttered Lia and shivered.

Sue-Ellen didn't say anything. She looked at Lia. She saw that Lia like herself had breasts forming, that she looked white and soft under her clothes though still speckled with a myriad of freckles like a fine cinnamon dusting all over her.

Lia felt Sue-Ellen's eyes and swallowed. Swiftly she looked back. She saw Sue-Ellen's strong free legs dangling in the water, saw the fine pubic hair just forming and the bands of white skin next to the sun-tanned places.

"You're sure pretty," said Sue-Ellen. "Your hair seems like it was on fire."

Lia smiled. "Thank you," she murmured.

"What're them silver things on your teeth?" asked Sue-Ellen pointing. She'd been wanting to ask a long time and now she felt full of questions and curiosity. She wanted to know all the things about Lia she'd never dared to ask before.

"Oh them. They're for straightening my teeth." Lia swallowed and looked down. Suddenly she felt sad. She frowned and thought about home.

"My family don't think I'm pretty," she said at last.

"Certain, they're wrong," said Sue-Ellen hotly.

"You tell them," said Lia in a weary voice. "They're always trying to stuff me into uncomfortable clothes or make me over like I was some kind of thing."

Sue-Ellen didn't answer. She frowned into the water and looked at Lia from the corner of her eye. Suddenly she had to know.

"Lia," she said. "Lia, you think I'm pretty?"

64

There was silence. It seemed as if the light shifted a little around them, as if time slid out of focus and stood still for a moment, as if they were set apart in something old, a ritual, a first knowing.

Lia looked up because she felt the urgency in Sue-Ellen's voice. She gazed at Sue-Ellen long and hard. Lia saw the other's breasts, pushing forward, round and firm almost like a woman's. Her eyes slid away. She felt they both must turn now, run each a separate way. But they didn't. Lia swallowed. She looked down, but she could still feel Sue-Ellen's wide and urgent eyes.

"Yes, Sue-Ellen, you're pretty. You're, well, awful grown up."

And somehow her friend did seem beyond reach, clothed in that mature nakedness.

But Sue-Ellen's face broke into a grin of relief. "I ain't that grown up," she said. "Have you started yet? I mean bleeding and such as Granny told me of."

Lia shook her head.

"Neither have I," said Sue-Ellen and suddenly their lips quivered. They giggled in embarrassment. Then they both laughed, heads back, somehow free now. Lia gave Sue-Ellen a big push into the slow dark water. She jumped in after. They scuffled playfully, bare arms and legs warm as they touched. They plunged and splashed in the brook until both had

65

ducked the other. Then they bounded out of the dark water into the light and softness of the woods, snorting and sniffing with life.

X

It was late afternoon. Lia held Noni softly in her arms. Nearby Sue-Ellen sat. It had been a rich full day. Lia looked down the wooded hill and towards the stone house she couldn't see. A dark worry lay in the pit of her stomach. Soon she had to go home. Lia held Noni closer, not wanting the time to pass, not wanting to change anything.

Sue-Ellen stirred. She cleared her throat. "I reckon," she began uneasily. "I reckon Granny'll be lookin' for me."

Lia closed her eyes and swallowed.

"Supposin', I mean, would you be comin' up in the morning?"

Lia nodded and bit her lip.

"Well then . . ." Sue-Ellen stood and moved a tentative step. "I'll be goin' then, I reckon." She walked slowly, turning her head towards Lia from time to time.

Suddenly Lia twisted around. "Bye!" she cried loudly, urgently.

"Bye!" Sue-Ellen raised her hand and then swiftly raced off, not able to be held any longer.

Lia ducked her head. She heard the twigs breaking underfoot. She closed her eyes. The stillness seemed complete. Then she heard the twigs breaking again. Was Sue-Ellen returning? She looked up hopefully.

"Billy!" Lia's heart lurched inside her. She stood up clutching Noni.

"Is she gone?" asked Billy.

"Who?" Lia tried to make her face blank while fear leaped up in her throat like a fiery fluid.

"Stop pretending. I saw her. Dad's been looking for you. He's worried and mad. What on earth did you say this morning?"

"I'm not going home," said Lia and looked away. "I can't go ever."

"Don't be a twirp. He'd find you. In fact, I'd tell him where to look."

"You wouldn't dare." Lia's face twisted. She raised her fist.

"Lia, come on." Billy pushed her gently. "You haven't got a chance fighting me."

Lia looked down. Her stomach felt as if it were boiling. She opened her mouth and closed it. Suddenly she looked at Billy. Her blue eyes opened wide.

"I'll come," she said fiercely, "if you promise never to tell you saw her. Swear it! Never tell about her or Noni or this tree or anything. Swear! Swear!

At first Billy wanted to laugh, but Lia's face was so intense, so full of pain and worry, he had to nod instead.

"I swear."

Then wordlessly, tenderly, Lia placed Noni in the tree and went down the hill behind her brother like a shadow.

Lia found it strange at home. She slid through the door behind Billy. Mother came to the hall.

"There you are," she said lightly. "Better have a bath before dinner."

In the living room Father shifted his weight in his easy chair. No one spoke to her of the morning's outburst. Only Mrs. Stark said something about the torn and dirty dress. It was as if no one would admit something unpleasant had happened. Lia felt more like a stranger than ever. She escaped upstairs, chilled, as if someone had shut all the doors to the house and left her out in a wind.

It was a little different at the dinner table. Father looked at her searchingly. His big bushy eyebrows hid his eyes and Lia felt fear coiling like a snake in her stomach.

"You had some strong opinions this morning, young lady," he said and his voice rolled like a heavy stone down a paved path.

"William dear, it is lonely for the children," Mother interrupted. "You were so clever to think of the Symonsons. I called and they'll be delighted to come in a couple of weeks." Mother spoke rapidly. Her face grew flushed with effort. "Everything will be so gay and pleasant. You'll see. Really!"

Lia stared at the green beans on her plate. Father looked at Mother and cleared his throat. Slowly he looked away. "I'll be going back to the office to-morrow," he declared abruptly.

"Oh," Mother's eyes widened. A little hurt look escaped across her face. Then she grasped the meat platter. "William," she said, "won't you have some more lamb?" Her voice was just right, tuned to some-thing distant, perfect and untouchable.

Lia swallowed and thought of Noni, thought of the comfortable silence that spoke louder than words around Sue-Ellen's worn kitchen table. She sighed and ate her cold green beans one by one.

XI

FOR LIA THE WEEKS FLEW by because she was able to run off up into the woods. There the days passed in a kind of dreamlike way. But now Sue-Ellen would sometimes venture closer to the stone house, waiting for Lia to come and wondering what lay behind the well-placed fieldstone walls. Why did Lia never ask her in? Perhaps there was something still, something that made Sue-Ellen not good enough? Lia always pulled her away from the sight of the house, hurried her off to the woods, not seeming at ease until they were deep among the trees.

Sue-Ellen puzzled, but then she forgot because the

game at hand caught them both up in an intense and joyful world. They followed chipmunks to their holes, watched snakes baking in the sun. They found nests full of eggs, and a family of porcupines. It was as if the world were flowering, burgeoning and they were in the center: fed by sunlight, sheltered by leaves, carressed by the wind, entertained by ants, beetles, moles, rabbits, thrushes and skylarks. Time stood still.

Only it didn't. At home Lia's mother was preparing for the Symonsons. And whenever she could she cornered Lia.

"Jeannette will want to sleep in your room, dearest. Or perhaps we should put her in the yellow guest room? It's so sunny there. What do you think?"

Lia shrugged. She couldn't imagine an answer. Jeannette wasn't real. Nothing in the house was real. And it bothered Lia when Sue-Ellen asked about the house, about Mother and Father.

"Let's not talk about it," Lia would say quickly. "Is your Granny making bread? Can we have some? Can we swim, Sue-Ellen? Come on, let's get away from here. It's too close to the house."

Sue-Ellen wanted to stop her, wanted to ask, "Is it on account your house is too good for the likes of me?" But she didn't dare because she saw Lia's eager face, saw the quick, lopsided smile, saw the urgency in Lia's eyes. And so again they plunged into the thickets to be lost in another day.

Lia saw the big gray car draw up. Somewhere in the back seat she saw Jeannette's head bobbing like something lost in a vast sea. It was midmorning. Lia swallowed and glanced out towards the meadow. Somewhere in the woods Sue-Ellen waited. And Lia hadn't told her about Jeannette yet! Somehow Lia hadn't been able to bring herself to talk about anything to do with the house. Now she stood, shifting on her feet, biting her lip and worrying. What would Sue-Ellen think when Lia didn't come?

"How nice to see you. We're so delighted!" Mother's greeting fluted on the morning air. "And Jeannette, how lovely you look. And how you've grown! Lia, come here, dear."

Lia shook hands with Mr. and Mrs. Symonson and bobbed a quick curtsy. Then she glanced at Jeannette. Her old friend was all clothes—beautiful tailored clothes out of which she peered with a lost bewildered look like a dog caught in a child's game of dress-up. Even her hair was groomed with a rhinestone studded ribbon like a poodle's collar. Lia had to look away. She could barely manage a mumbled, "Hi."

But Mother rushed on, filling the silence. "And

how was your trip? Easy, I hope. Billy, take the luggage, won't you dear? William, will come late this afternoon. He'll be so pleased to see you."

Jeannette sniffed the air. She looked around with a frown as if to hide the way her eyes darted around uneasily. "What do you do around here?" she asked.

Lia shrugged. "Things," she answered.

"Oh!" said Jeannette and it almost sounded like a little whimper. "Well, then it's lucky I brought my ouija board," she declared, holding tightly to her overnight bag.

"Where would you like to sleep?" asked Lia. "In my room or in the yellow guest room? The guest room is really nicer," she rushed to add. "Lots of sun and pretty wall paper. You can have a bathroom all to yourself. You'd like it."

"I'll take your word for it," said Jeannette and took dainty awkward steps over the threshold on her shiny pumps.

Lia sighed, gazed quickly towards the distant elms, and followed Jeannette inside.

XII

Why didn't lia come? Sue-Ellen chafed as she sat and waited beneath their tree. She pulled Noni out of his hollow and stared at the gray bundle. It looked so helpless and vulnerable, like something thrown away. Sue-Ellen held it the way Lia did. It was soft, not unpleasant. But it didn't bring her comfort the way it did Lia. Still it was something Lia loved, something of her life they shared. Sue-Ellen gave the owl a soft little pat and put it back in the tree. She stared down the wooded hills and knew how much she missed Lia.

Days back Granny had guessed how much Sue-Ellen cared even when she herself didn't want to admit it. Why didn't Lia come? What was keeping her? Should Sue-Ellen go down by the fence and see? Would she even dare go all the way to the house?

Uncertainly Sue-Ellen waited. The time crept by. At last she rose. She had to go and see. Already it was noontime. Granny would wonder where she was, but she just had to find it all out. Sue-Ellen began to run, slowly at first, then faster, pounding through the underbrush until she stood, out of breath, by the fence edging the meadow.

There Sue-Ellen saw the big gray car parked by the house. No one was outside. Sue-Ellen stood feeling her own heart bang. Would she dare go all the way to the house? Would she dare? Sue-Ellen swallowed. What would Lia say? She'd come to the door, wouldn't she? She'd ask Sue-Ellen in at last, wouldn't she? Surely, they were real friends now.

Cautiously, gingerly, Sue-Ellen emerged from the elms and swung herself over the fence. How long the meadow seemed, stretched before her to the house. Acres and acres of openness. Sue-Ellen shivered. But she kept on going and no one came. Nothing stirred except the red clover in the wind and the buttercups just coming up after the first mowing.

At last Sue-Ellen approached the front door of the stone house. She felt a deep panic, a fright that held her stiff before the big, shiny, brass knocker. Lia had to be inside! She had to come to the door! Slowly, almost shutting her eyes, Sue-Ellen raised the knocker. It fell against the door with a sound like a pistol.

"Now who could that be?" said Mother a little startled. She spoke to everyone assembled in the living room. "Not William surely. He's not due till later. And luncheon will be served in another moment or two. We're not expecting anyone."

She rose from her chintz chair and glided to the door. There was a soft murmuring. Then Mother called.

"Lia, dear, there's someone here to see you. She *says* she knows you."

Holding Sue-Ellen a bit at a distance Mother brought her in to the edge of the living room.

Sue-Ellen looked wildly around trying to find Lia. Lia saw her friend and turned pale. Lia's eyes raced to Mother. She saw Mother's disapproving stare at Sue-Ellen's bare feet, at her disheveled shirt. Lia saw Jeannette's uneasy look, saw her drawing back deep into the sofa for safety.

"Lia, do you know this person?" asked Mother, her voice rising sharply.

Lia stood up. She couldn't open her mouth.
"Well?"
Lia stammered. "No, Mother . . . no, I never saw

her before. I don't know who she is. I don't know what she wants . . ." Lia looked down and away.

Sue-Ellen's eyes widened, turned dark like the brook water. She spun on her feet and fled silently past Mother.

XIII

"MY GRACIOUS," said Mother and shut the door. "One of the natives, I imagine. She thought she could get in here with a trick like that. Well, let's not let it bother us. Shall we go to lunch?"

Lia stood staring at the floor. She suddenly felt ill. What had she done? How could she have said that? Lia's fingers felt icy, as if they'd drop off one by one. Sue-Ellen's widening eyes rushed by in her mind. And Lia's own words fell relentlessly on her ear. "I never saw her before. I don't know who she is . . ."

Lia wanted suddenly to cry out. Her face felt drawn and stretched out of shape. How could she have said that?

Through the living room to the dining room the Symonsons trooped. Jeannette brushed past Lia.

"Did you see her?" she said with a little nervous tremor. "There has to be a lot of weirdos around here."

Lia stared at Jeannette. She swallowed rapidly. "Yes," she said hotly. "A lot!" And Lia turned towards the door.

"Hurry, Lia, dear!" called Mother glancing quickly at her daughter. "Lunch time!"

But Lia didn't answer. She opened the door. Mother hurried over.

"Now, Lia. There's no need to pay attention to someone who comes barging into this house like that. Thank heavens she had sense to leave. Come along."

"No," said Lia, and her face was white and thin as a new moon. "No. No."

"Don't be silly. What will the Symonsons think?" Mother's face clouded with little dark frowns.

"I don't care what the Symonsons think." Lia's voice rose. "I don't care what *you* think. I don't care what anybody thinks."

Then she ran through the door and across the endless meadow into the woods.

"Sue-Ellen! SUE-ELLEN!" Lia called herself hoarse while she plunged through the underbrush.

The woods reverberated with noise. Lia looked everywhere. She peered under thickets. She looked behind boulders and trees. She searched the little dells.

In the hollow of the tree, Noni was left untouched. There was no one there. The raspberry patch was empty except for the droning of bees.

Lia began to feel desperate. The tears came pushing up, tears of remorse and sorrow.

"Sue-Ellen! Sue-Ellen! PLEASE!" Lia burst into tears. She sat in the late afternoon light and cried the whole misery out.

It grew quiet around her. Lia drew a deep breath. She felt empty as if she would echo hollow when she walked. For a long time she sat dumb and mindless, watching the light change. Then slowly Lia became more aware of the woods, the wind in the trees, the silence around her.

Thank heavens no one had followed her from the house. It was a relief. She knew Mother would worry about what the Symonsons thought and no one would go chasing after her. That gave Lia time.

She rose. Sue-Ellen would have gone home to Granny, wouldn't she? Why had Lia not thought of it? She bit her lip. It was because she hadn't wanted to look there, hadn't wanted Granny to know and to despise her.

Lia shook herself. Still, she had to go there. Slowly

Lia turned and climbed the ridges. The early evening light fell softly over the high meadow that rose above her. Lia started up the narrow path. Soon she began to run.

"Sue-Ellen!" she called. "Sue-Ellen!"

She plunged into the yard and up on to the porch. Granny looked through the screen door. Her old face was creased like a rumpled paper.

"Child, what's happened to Sue-Ellen?" asked Granny with concern as she opened the screen door.

"I don't know. Isn't she here?" asked Lia.

"No. She ain't been up to the house all day. I thought she might be down to your place."

"She was," whispered Lia and tears welled forward. "Granny, I . . . oh, I can't tell you."

"Reckon there was trouble then," said Granny a little grimly.

Lia nodded. "It was my fault. Granny. And I have to find her. I've looked everywhere. I've called and called. She doesn't answer. Oh, I feel so terrible I could die."

"The hurts as you give can sometimes pain the most," murmured Granny and came slowly outside.

"But what shall I do?"

"She'll be comin' back, I reckon," said Granny.

"But I want to find her. To tell her . . . to . . . oh, it's awful."

Granny nodded softly. "You might look up that there road," she said, pointing slowly. "There's an old place for the cows to pass under the road. No one uses it now. Sue-Ellen, she still has a fancy for that place."

Lia rose. "Thank you, Granny," she said and tore off.

"I hope you'll come back, child!" called Granny after her. Then slowly she went to wait in the old rocker.

XIV

THE LIGHT WAS DIM NOW. Lia hurried up the dark road. One evening star blinked in the gray-blue sky and the pines closed in around her. The hill rose steadily. An old pasture with a broken gate lay to her right. The ruts in the road were like deep valleys. Lia stumbled, but she went on, hearing her own breath mark the time and the distance. The road seemed to go on endlessly.

At last she saw a bend in the road. It seemed as if a large culvert lay under the road. Lia stopped. Her stomach pinched with sudden dread. Was this the place? She edged closer, moving off the road and crawling through the tangle of weeds and stones.

She entered the underpass. It was made of square stones vaulting under the road. It was narrow, cold and dark inside.

"Sue-Ellen?" whispered Lia. Was there a shadow at the other opening? "Sue-Ellen," whispered Lia and her voice bounced against the dark granite walls. "Please . . . I want to . . ."

The shadow stirred and darted out into the night. Lia saw it was Sue-Ellen and plunged after her. She made a quick desperate grab for Sue-Ellen's arm.

"Sue-Ellen, I didn't mean what I said," Lia blurted out breathlessly while holding on. "I didn't want to hurt you. Oh, please, listen. I wanted you to be my secret. I didn't want any one to know about you be-cause . . . because I like you so much. It's like . . . like Noni. They'd take you away. I know they would. Please, Sue-Ellen. Please, listen."

Sue-Ellen twisted free and stood fiercely still. Her breath came in little pants. Then she wiped jerkily at her tear-streaked face.

"Granny told me to look for you here," Lia rushed on, hoping to hold her with words, words that tumbled out. "Sue-Ellen," Lia caught her friend's hand tight. "I'm sorry, Sue-Ellen. Please, I . . . I . . ." Lia couldn't finish. It was as if words were just bits of emptiness in the night air. Nothing would change what had happened. Lia dropped Sue-Ellen's hand.

"I don't blame you," said Lia tiredly and turned to go.

Down the hill she walked silently, not thinking, not knowing where to go, not letting herself feel. Lia walked alone. The slope of the hill unrolled before her, taking her down, down. Now she heard Sue-Ellen's feet slapping behind her. Lia crossed into the rut on one side of the road and walked on, not looking back.

Now Sue-Ellen walked alongside her in the other rut. Their feet made quick anxious patter, crunching the gravel underfoot. They went on and on, two separate shadows.

They didn't speak. Ahead Lia could see the light in Granny's kitchen. Before long they would be abreast of the brook and the open yard and the meadow below the house. Lia pushed on. She wouldn't stop. She'd go right on. It was all too late. Nothing could change.

At the house she turned towards Sue-Ellen.

"Good-bye," she said quickly and then she darted away past the chicken run and down the narrow path in the meadow.

Sue-Ellen gave a startled little movement. She stood suspended on the porch step, surrounded by her own silence like a larva in its own fine silk. Below she saw Lia's shape fade off.

"Lia," she whispered. Her friend was out of sight. "Lia." Her voice rose. "Lia! LIA!"

Sue-Ellen broke from the safety of the porch and dashed down the meadow. She ignored the path and plunged through the grass, rising on strong legs, leaping forward over the height of the wild wheat, over the breadth of her own resistance, over the length of the distance between them.

"Lia! Lia!"

She stopped in front of her friend, gulping for air. Then slowly, with a little tremble, she stretched her hand out and in the darkness, searched for Lia's.

XV

AFTER GREETING EVERYONE Father glanced around the living room.

"Where's Lia?" he asked looking at the Symonsons sitting with eyes half closed in the chintz sofas. In the dusky light of the evening they looked like part of the furniture.

"Where's Lia?" asked Father again, his voice booming.

No one answered.

Mother gave a little apologetic cough. "She went off suddenly. But we expect she'll be back any moment." Mother rubbed her long fingers together.

"That was an age ago," whined Jeannette from the

sofa before Mrs. Symonson could hush her up.

Father's head went up."What did you say?" he asked almost pouncing, though his voice was soft.

"Now, Jeannette," said Mr. Symonson in alarm. "You must be all wrong. It couldn't possibly have been that long ago."

"But it was!" whimpered Jeannette, looking red and disheveled in her beautiful clothes.

Father walked over to Mother.

"What have you done about it?" he asked softly.

"Nothing, dear." Mother's face went white. "I couldn't really with guests. And . . . well, I thought surely she'd come straight back."

Father stood in the living room like a great hulking light house and turned to stare at each one there. Behind him in the window the darkness of the sky joined the dark rim of the distant trees.

"Good God," he said at last, staring at everyone. "Great good God!"

Father barreled out into the dusky light. "Lia!" he called bellowing out over the meadow, out over the woods. "Lia . . . L - I - A - A - A - H!"

Mother ran out to him. "William!" she said, laying her fluttering white hands like moth wings on his arm. "William, really she must be . . ."

"How long has Lia been gone?" he demanded shaking Mother. "How long?"

"Since lunch, I think. But surely . . ."

Father's face was white and drawn. "The child was right," he said almost in a whisper. "Nobody knows who anybody is in this family . . ." Father stared at Mother. "Everybody's going to look for that child, do you hear?"

"But what about the Symonsons?"

"Send them home!" roared Father.

"But dear, we can't really. We . . ."

"If you can't, I will," said Father and charged into the living room.

Half an hour later the gray car with the three Symonsons pulled jerkily away from the house, its white headlights backing into darkness like the eyes of some beast moving off into hiding.

Mother cried and leaned against the wall of the house while Billy stood silently apart.

Then Mrs. Stark, arms akimbo, appeared in the door. "Dinner is served," she called commandingly into the night air while above her the moths danced around the front door light.

"Shut up!" roared Father.

In the silence that followed Mother's faint sobs could be heard joining the sounds of the insects in the night and the uneasy crunch of Billy's feet shifting in the gravel.

"Does anybody know where Lia is?" demanded Father. "You, Mrs. Stark?"

"I certainly do not," said Mrs. Stark sharply, still stinging from Father's recent roar. "I've said all along those children shouldn't be allowed in the woods. If they were mine, I wouldn't stand for it. Coming back looking like ruffians. No, Mr. Stratton, I haven't the slightest idea where Lia is."

"What about you?" asked Father, striding towards the house. He held Mother by the shoulder and shook her gently.

She made a futile gesture with her hand.

"Billy?" Father spun to face his son.

Billy swallowed. His eyes wanted to slide away from Father's bushy stare, the way they always had. But slowly he made himself meet Father's eyes. Billy wiped his clammy hands along his pants.

"I—I'll help you look," he said in a rush to keep his voice from shaking.

"Well, I need you," Father said simply with a nod. It was a formal gesture, one of recognition, and Billy's heart pounded. Suddenly he couldn't stand still. He had to dash off for his flashlight, had to run because a swift and crazy joy was flowing inside him.

XVI

THEY WALKED SIDE BY SIDE IN SILENCE. Ahead, the wavering white spot made by the flashlight bound them together. They were in the denser darkness of the woods now. Father's breath came fast and heavy as they climbed. Only the crunch of their feet broke the stillness. Steadily they pushed on. The thickets closed behind them and there was the occasional scuttle of a startled animal. They went on and on.

At last Billy stopped and shined the flashlight around, marking a place.

"She comes here a lot," he said finally. "I thought maybe we'd find her."

Father blinked and looked at the place. "What's here?" he asked, puzzled, and a little out of breath.

Silently Billy reached into the hollow of a tree and brought out Noni. He held the old stuffed toy out to Father who took it and looked at it intently. Then he gazed at Billy questioningly.

Billy hesitated. "It's something . . . well, secret, she keeps."

Father looked at Noni again. Then determinedly he buttoned the old owl into his coat. "O.K., where to?"

Billy opened his hands uncertainly. "Well, I'm not sure I should tell," he said. "It's well . . ."

Father waited and Billy circled the ground with the flashlight.

"She's got a friend," Billy blurted out at last. "I saw her once. She must live up that way." Billy pointed with the light. "And I guess . . ."

Father was already off and Billy had to plunge after him. They climbed the dark and silent ridges. The big hulk of the man pressed on like a huge ship at sea while the boy bobbed behind him, a small dinghy.

They didn't speak until they emerged at the edge of the rising meadow. Above them a single light shone in an old house.

"Is that it?" asked Father.

94

Billy swallowed. "I guess," he said.

"You guess, eh?" uneasy, Father laughed. "O.K.," he said a little uncertainly. "Let's go."

They dove into the meadow, swimming through the deep grass and emerging at last by the old porch. Father's step fell heavily on the old boards. A hen scurried across the chicken run. Father raised his big red hand and pounded on the screen door. There was a stirring within. They waited.

Slowly the door was opened and an old woman appeared.

"Yes?" she asked, cocking her head to one side.

Father gazed at her. Slowly he lowered his hand that was ready to knock again.

"Is my daughter here?" he asked gentling his voice.

The old woman squinted. She looked at him steadily. Satisfied, she slowly nodded her head. "If you be meanin' Lia, then she's here."

Father's face broke into a grin. He sighed with relief.

"Well, I've come for her," he said. "Please send her out."

The woman shook her head slowly. "Maybe you'd best ask if she's ready to go."

Father opened his mouth. Then he closed it as suddenly. He turned to Billy.

"Can you make it home alone, Billy?" he asked.

Billy swallowed. "Well, sure, I think I can."

"I'd appreciate it if you'd tell Mother we've found her. I'll be along later." Father held him by the shoulders a moment. "And thanks, son," he said quickly.

"O.K." Billy scuttled away, the light disappearing with him in the night.

"May I come in?" asked Father.

The old woman nodded. "I reckon you may now," she said and stepped solemnly back into the lighted house.

XVII

LIA SAW FATHER enter the room ducking his head through the low screen door. His eyes searched for her. Quickly Lia looked down. She felt her legs go tense and her fingers stiffen the way they did in the cold.

Father went over to her. He put a great heavy hand on her shoulders.

"It's time to go, Lia," he said. "These people have been kind long enough . . ."

Lia felt the weight of Father's hand. She wanted to wriggle free of it, but it lay there heavy and unavoidable. At last she looked up at Father for a fleeting moment.

"I don't want to go," she said almost soundlessly.

Father stood uneasily. He lifted his hands from Lia's shoulder. "I know you don't want to go," he said and looked around, noticing the worn shabbiness of the old house, the bare floors, the nicked chairs and table. He spread his hands and laughed a small uncomfortable laugh. "But you can't impose here any longer."

Then Lia's eyes blazed. "Don't laugh!" she said fiercely. "Don't you laugh at Sue-Ellen and Granny. They're . . . they're better than lots of people I know."

"Of course, they are," said Father. He stepped back, smiling and glancing at Sue-Ellen in the corner. Then quickly he felt for his back pocket and turned to Granny. Lia saw that he was flustered.

"I very much appreciate your taking my daughter in like this." He dug in his pocket and was able to extricate his wallet at last. "I'd like to show my appreciation," he said giving an embarrassed grin. Hurriedly Father picked some money from his wallet.

Lia's face turned white.

"*No!*" she said, hurtling across the room and grabbing Father's arm. "*No! No!* You aren't buying them. *No!*" Her face twisted. "You've bought everything. You've put everything in a cage. *No!*" She

99

yanked at him, clawing at his hand, until the wallet fell to the floor.

Father's face turned quite red. He looked at Lia with a hurt bewildered stare. Lia swallowed. Quickly she dropped to the floor and retrieved the wallet. She gave it to Father and hurried across to the rocker while her eyes filled up with tears. Father stood silent, his powerful arms useless along his sides. No one said anything. Only Lia's crying was heard like a soft whisper from the old rocker.

Then Granny rose slowly. "I reckon it's time for some coffee. I feel the use of it now. Sue-Ellen, child, go for the milk."

Sue-Ellen scurried out, letting a soft night breeze in through the door.

"Won't you be stayin' for a cup then?" Granny asked, eyeing Father slowly.

Father looked at Lia huddled in the rocker. "Yes," he said wearily and cleared his throat. "I'd . . . I'd like that."

"So. . . ." said Granny and ambled to the kitchen with her aged walk.

They were left in the room by themselves. Father looked uneasily at Lia. He took a step towards her. Then feeling within his jacket he pulled out Noni.

"Lia," he said. "Here, I have something for you."

"I don't want it!" cried Lia, not looking up. "I

don't want anything."

"But it belongs to you," said Father and walked to the rocker. "Here." He put the old stuffed toy by her side.

Eyes closed, Lia's hand went out. She touched the familiar matted fur and she froze.

Father looked away. He turned his back to the rocker and gazed out the window.

"Billy showed me where it was," said Father, explaining. "He said it was special to you. I thought maybe you'd like to have it."

Lia didn't answer. Clasping Noni tightly to her she watched Father anxiously.

He sighed and touched the scarred kitchen table. He let his gaze fall to the worn wood.

"I haven't seen a table like this since I was a boy," he said softly. "A sturdy 'no account' table. Like your toy there, Lia. Maybe it's the 'no account' part that makes it special. The feeling about it doesn't seem to wear out somehow." He turned towards Lia, taking hesitant steps.

"Child . . ." He reached a big clumsy hand towards her and mussed her red hair. Softly, deeply, he chuckled where the sound was tears and smiles both. "Who'd have thought you were such a fierce one?" He patted her awkwardly on the top of her head. "I guess I haven't taken the time to see you truly."

From deep within the rocker Lia let out a soft little sound. It was like air escaping from deep mud, rising, rising to a watery surface with a small clear bubble and a hiss of relief. She looked up at Father and slowly let her lips quiver into a shy and fleeting smile.

XVIII

THEY'D SAT A LONG TIME OVER COFFEE. The steaming smell and the soft light in the kitchen bound them gently.

Granny chuckled at Father's stories of his youth, nodding her wispy head of hair in recognition while Sue-Ellen and Lia sat close to each other watching. Outside the sky was bright and clear, the stars hanging low and almost reachable.

At last it was time to go. Father rose and bowed to Granny.

"Thank you," he said simply.

Granny nodded while a little toothless smile erupted. Father turned to Sue-Ellen.

"I know Lia would like to have you come to visit

if you would," Father glanced searchingly towards Lia. "So come down when you want to," he finished hurriedly.

Lia stared and swallowed. Had Father forgotten Mother? Had he forgotten Mrs. Stark and all the things that had happened? Lia swallowed. She murmured her goodbyes along with Father, trying not to think, trying not to worry, intent only on getting away.

Once outside, the night air rushed over her along with doubts and fearfulness. If Sue-Ellen came again, what would Mother say? What would happen then?

Lia began to run, holding Noni tightly. Father lumbered behind, down, down over the meadow to the edge of the woods. She stopped, waiting for Father to catch up. She turned on him, not able to keep her worry secret.

"Why'd you ask Sue-Ellen to come? You know Mother won't have her." Lia's voice rose. "You know she'll . . . she'll . . . she'll only say something awful . . . and she might be . . . might be on those pills and . . ." There, she had said it. And now her tongue burned in her mouth.

Father was silent. Lia waited anxiously. Why didn't he speak? He just stood in the dark and shifted his feet. At last he cleared his throat. "Maybe she would at that," Father said sadly. He sighed and turned towards her. "The pills are no secret to you then, Lia?"

Lia shook her head.

"It's been worrying you about Mother, hasn't it?"

Lia looked down. The silence lay like a dead weight on her. Then Father let his breath out in a long and shaky sort of way.

"I don't know that we can do anything about the pills, Lia," he said finally. "It's Mother who has to do something about them."

The night wrapped them each into darkness. Then slowly Father reached his hand out and touched Lia's shoulder. "Still, Lia," he said, "when it comes to all of us being together, something new might happen." He waited a moment. "You know, even strangers speak to each other sometime. And birds in a cage sing, if you listen. So who knows, Lia?"

He turned to her intently. "I can't promise anything, but I'll have a talk with Mother about Sue-Ellen. And then I think maybe, maybe we ought to give it a chance, what do you say?"

Lia stood silently at the edge of the woods. Suddenly she reached out and touched Father, too, not saying anything. They stood a moment like that, watching the stars' slow wheeling in the sky.

Lia took a step. "Wait a minute," she said. "Wait for me." And she rushed back up the meadow,

leaping into the darkness and the tall grass. She didn't stop until she stood on the porch of the old house.

Drawing a breath, Lia knocked. Slowly Sue-Ellen came to the door and opened it.

"Here!" Lia stretched out her hand with Noni in it. "I want you to have it," she said, holding the toy out. "I want you to have it because it's special."

Wordlessly Sue-Ellen took the owl. Lia stood a moment looking at her friend, then she had to dash away. In the yard she turned.

"Could you come tomorrow? Could you come? . . ." Lia's voice broke off.

Sue-Ellen stood in the doorway. Her heart pounded. The silence lay waiting between them. Slowly Sue-Ellen stirred. Holding Noni she opened the door farther.

"I reckon!" she called softly. Then louder. "I reckon I could."

Lia laughed. It was a quick high sound of expectancy. She dashed off, barreling down through the long grass, flinging her arms out in a free-wheeling circle.

"YOO-HOO!" she called into the lifting darkness around her.

An answer followed her from the house. And from the edge of the woods an answer met her.

"YOO-HOO! . . . YOO-HOO!"